On Uncle John's Farm

To Kyle and Kirsti, who share farm memories with me
and to Ann Featherstone, who has never ceased to be a supportive and constructive editor and friend
and to Gail Winskill, for believing in this story

—Sally

To my daughter, Arielle
and with a merci to Alyssa

—Brian

Text copyright © 2005 by Sally Fitz-Gibbon
Illustration copyright © 2005 by Brian Deines

Fitzhenry & Whiteside,
195 Allstate Parkway, Markham, Ontario L3R 4T8

In the United States,
121 Harvard Avenue, Suite 2, Allston, Massachusetts 02134

www.fitzhenry.ca   godwit@fitzhenry.ca.

10 9 8 7 6 5 4 3 2 1

National Library of Canada Cataloguing in Publication

Fitz-Gibbon, Sally, 1949-
On Uncle John's farm / Sally Fitz-Gibbon ; illustrations by Brian Deines.

ISBN 1-55041-691-X (bound).—ISBN 1-55041-886-6 (pbk.)

1. Farm life—Juvenile fiction. I. Deines, Brian II. Title.

PS8561.I87O5 2003   jC813'.54   C2003-902333-8
PZ7

U.S. Publisher Cataloging-in-Publication Data
(Library of Congress Standards)

Fitz-Gibbon, Sally.
On Uncle John's farm / Sally Fitz-Gibbon ; Brian Deines. —1st ed.
[32] p. : col. ill. ; cm.
Summary: Describes all the excitement for children of being on a farm.
ISBN 1-55041-691-X
ISBN 1-55041-886-6 (pbk.)
1. Farms — Fiction — Juvenile literature. 2. Family farms — Fiction — Juvenile literature.
(1. Farms — Fiction. 2. Farm life — Fiction.)
I. Deines, Brian. II. Title.
[E] 21   PZ7.F589On 2003

Fitzhenry & Whiteside acknowledges with thanks the Canada Council for the Arts, the Government of Canada through the Book Publishing Industry Development Program (BPIDP), the Ontario Arts Council and the Government of Ontario through the Ontario Media Development Corporation's Ontario Book Initiative for their support for our publishing program.

Design by Wycliffe Smith

Printed in Hong Kong

On Uncle John's Farm

by Sally Fitz-Gibbon
Pictures by Brian Deines

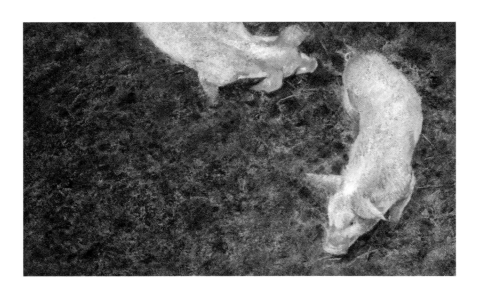

Fitzhenry & Whiteside

On Uncle John's farm I wake up in a hurry,

tangled in blankets, I land on the floor.

Struggling with tee shirt and socks, I go sliding

over to windows and open them wide.

Leaning out, laughing, I waken a robin

sitting so silently still in her nest.

And I see below me a play-tiny farmyard,

with finger-sized horses and

button-small sheep.

I run to the stairway and clatter down loudly.

Leaping and laughing, I follow my nose

to warm smells of bacon and syrup and coffee,

to arms that hug tightly and welcome me in.

Licking my fingers and listening to voices,

I wriggle and squiggle and slide from my chair.

Uncle John scoops me and carries me, giggling,

out to the farmyard to start a new day.

On Uncle John's farm

we pass puddles of ducklings

with smiles on their faces and curls in their tails.

A rooster walks stiffly on stilt-legs with ruffles,

calling to hens to keep out of our way.

We follow the pathway that leads to the pigpens where piglets on tiptoe play **Follow the Leader.** Snuffling and smiling, they circle their mothers lying like puddings in thick chocolate sauce.

On Uncle John's farm

    there's a barn built for hiding,

filled full of kittens that squirm in my arms.

I climb up the ladders and hide in the hay bales,

while Uncle John scratches his head

    and looks lost.

On Uncle John's farm

    there are cousins like giants.

I hear them come calling me,

    "FEE-FIE-FO-FUM!"

They rush up the ladder and search

    till they find me,

then, tickling, they toss me high into the air.

We crowd in the wagon behind the red tractor,

and Uncle John drives us out into the fields

where sky-high corn opens and closes behind us,

and only the swallows can see where we are.

I lie in the sunshine on green piles of sweet corn,

feeling the rumbling of wheels going round.

Then Uncle John lets me drive home

    through the meadows,

and I hold the steering wheel tighter than tight.

Back in the garden of peas, beans, and carrots,

of strawberries staining my fingers and mouth,

I twirl in the middle of cabbage and lettuce,

my toes in the deep earth,

my arms to the breeze.

On Uncle John's farm we have supper together,

all of us eating rich dumplings and stew.

The clinking of soup spoons on thick china dishes

fills up my ears with their comforting sounds.

Out on the porch I sit, creaking in wicker,

toes pulling warmth from the

   paint-peeling boards.

The murmur and hum of the voices float by me.

Nodding and dozing, I curl in my chair.

Later, much later, in sea-deep white bathtub,

rough flannel fights with the dirt of the day.

Drying, I stand wrapped from nose-tip to toe-tips

in thick, puffy towels that smell fresh

from the line.

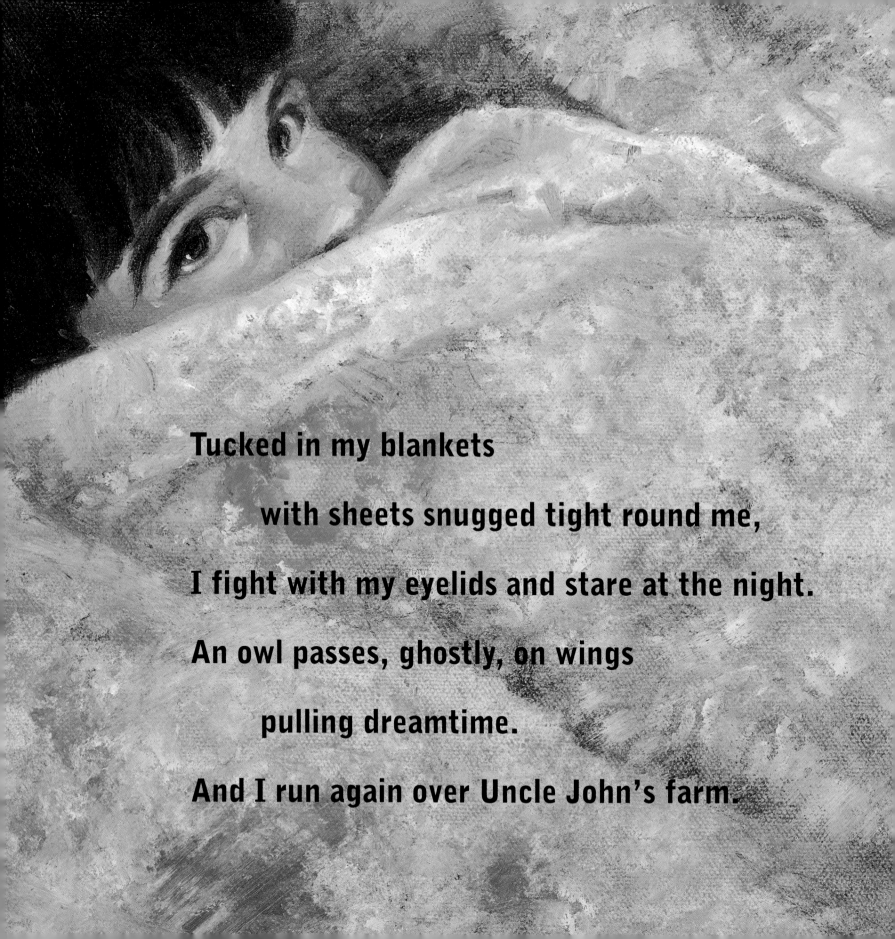

Tucked in my blankets

    with sheets snugged tight round me,

I fight with my eyelids and stare at the night.

An owl passes, ghostly, on wings

    pulling dreamtime.

And I run again over Uncle John's farm.